To order additional copies of this book, contact:
Xlibris
1-888-795-4274
www.Xlibris.com
Orders@Xlibris.com

Stacey F.

Blaque Diamond

Illustrations by Joel Ray Pellerin

It was a long car ride, and Stacey began to fall asleep in the back of her social worker, Mr. Jones car just as they arrived to the home of Ms. Grace.

"Good afternoon Ms. Grace," he said as he entered the home. This is Stacey.

"Delighted to meet you," Ms. Grace replied, as they walked into the dining room, to meet Ms. Grace's daughter, Paige.

"It's nice to meet you," said Paige. "This is Cleo the cat and Max our dog." "Purr," meowed Cleo the cat; "Ruff, ruff," barked Max the dog. "They like you," said Paige.

Before leaving Mr. Jones reminded Stacey of the letter Mrs. Penny put in her suitcase. Mrs. Penny wrote:

Dear Stacey,

As you read this letter I hope you know I am thinking of you and love you very much.

I know you will like your new family, and they will love you as much as I do.

Always,

Mrs. Penny

3

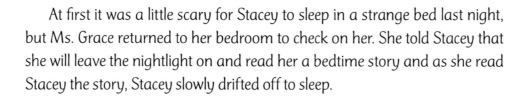

At first it was a little scary for Stacey to sleep in a strange bed last night, but Ms. Grace returned to her bedroom to check on her. She told Stacey that she will leave the nightlight on and read her a bedtime story and as she read Stacey the story, Stacey slowly drifted off to sleep.

The next morning she heard a knock on her bedroom door.

Knock, knock, knock!

"Come in, said Stacey." It was Paige.

"Everything is going to be all right," said Paige.

"How do you know?" replied Stacey

"I was afraid the first night I came as well," said Paige.

"Were you adopted too?" asked Stacey.

"No," replied Paige. "I am not Ms. Grace's real daughter, I am her foster daughter like you, but I will be going home soon.

"Where is home?" asked Stacey.

"Home is with my mother," said Paige.

Later that day, Ms. Grace received a call from Mr. Jones; he called to remind her of their next visit.

"I'll put a reminder on my calendar," said Ms. Grace.

"I will see you then," he said.

After talking to Mr. Jones, Ms. Grace decided to take Paige and Stacey to the flower shop. "They were going to introduce Stacey to Granny and take her some flowers.

"You will like Granny," said Paige. Granny is Ms. Grace's mother; she lives in a big house and she has a vegetable garden.

Paige knew Granny had a vegetable garden because she visits Granny quite often. But for Stacey, it will be her first visit. When they arrived Granny was working hard in her garden.

"Please come in," Granny said, as they walked on the stones to her garden. Welcome to my home.

As they handed Granny her flowers, they smelled Granny's cooking.

"I made fried tomatoes picked from my garden for lunch," said Granny.

6

After eating fried tomatoes, Granny told Stacey and Paige about a story of the city within the city. Granny and her parents lived in Manhattan, a borough in New York City.

"There are five boroughs in New York City," said Granny. "Brooklyn, Queens, The Bronx, Manhattan, and Staten Island, and someday I hope you can visit the big city."

"Is New York City far?" asked Paige.

"Not too Far." said Ms. Grace.

Just as Granny began to tell her story, it began to rain. Ms. Grace told Granny that it would be better if she finished the story the next time they visited her home.

"As they left Granny's home, they each thanked her for the tomatoes and she thanked them for her flowers.

"Paige was right; I did like Granny!" said Stacey. She is so soft and squishy. I hope the next time we visit Granny we can sit in her garden while she finishes the rest of the story about the city within the city.

"Granny tells the best stories," said Paige.

A few days later, Mr. Jones came for a visit. He said he was visiting Stacey to see how she was doing in her new home. Ms. Grace told him she was doing well and will be starting school soon.

"Would you like to see my new backpack," Stacey asked.

"Yes," replied Mr. Jones.

Stacey showed him her backpack, pencil case, notebook, and crayons. She even showed him her new lunchbox. While Mr. Jones and Ms. Grace spoke about the adoption Paige and Stacey were watching their favorite cartoon, Dream Girls. Mr. Jones explained that the next visit will be at his office with Mr. Waters for the service plan review.

"What is a service plan review?" asked Ms. Grace.

"A service plan review is a conference where we will plan for Stacey's future and well-being," he replied.

Ms. Grace asked, "Do you think Stacey will be adopted before the holidays?"

"No," Mr. Jones replied. "Stacey would need to be in your home for six months before the adoption can be legally finalized. In the meantime, I will continue to make home visits and keep you up to date with the adoption process."

After Mr. Jones left Ms. Grace took the girls shopping. Paige said "She likes to shop for the holidays," because it is her favorite time of the year and everything is bigger and brighter.

She is right. The lights are bright, and the trees are very big. You can even see the windows decorated with wreaths, garland, and Christmas ornaments, said Stacey.

"Tomorrow Ms. Grace will drive me to school. She said she had an early morning meeting to discuss my adoption with Mr. Waters and Mr. Jones," said Stacey.

Then she will meet with my social worker Mrs. Simpson. Mrs. Simpson will talk to my biological mother," said Paige.

"What is a biological mother?" Stacey asked.

"A biological mother is a Mother who gives birth to you," said Paige.

"Was Mrs. Penny my biological mother?" Stacey asked.

"No," said Paige, "she was your Foster Mother."

"Is Ms. Grace my biological mother?" Stacey asked.

"No," said Paige "she will be your Adoptive Mommy."

"What's the difference?" Stacey asked.

"Biological Mothers give birth to you. They love you unconditionally and sometimes have to make hard decisions," said Paige.

"And Mrs. Penny was your foster mother, and foster mothers make a choice. They love you and want to take care of you temporarily," said Paige.

"And Ms. Grace is your adoptive Mother, and adoptive mothers choose you. They love you, and they want to take care of you permanently," said Paige.

Ms. Grace took Stacey and Paige to her favorite Italian restaurant, Rigamonti's for dinner. The waiter took Stacey and Paige order of ravioli-Os, and Ms. Grace ordered stuffed shells. The waiter was a friend of Granny's. He said, "Ms. Grace used to come to the restaurant when she was a little girl."

"I remember when the waiter did not have a mustache," said Ms. Grace.

On the way home, Ms. Grace said they were going to stop for ice cream, but Stacey and Paige fell asleep in the car. When they awoke the next morning, Ms. Grace said they were going to visit Granny.

"I hope she will finish the story about the big city," said Paige.

"I hope she lets us plant in her garden," said Stacey.

"Whatever you girls do at Granny's house, I know you will have fun," said Ms. Grace.

When they arrived at Granny's house, Stacey and Paige ran into the kitchen to see Granny. She had cookies and milk waiting for them. As they ate their snack, Granny said she has a surprise for them.

"What is the surprise?" Stacey asked.

"You will have to wait until after you eat your snack," said Granny.

When they finished their cookies and milk, Granny took them to her favorite room in the house.

"Ms. Grace used to come in this room every Saturday when she was a little girl," said Granny.

"I wonder what is inside the room," said Paige.

It was Granny's sewing room! Granny had a sewing table—buttons, yarn, ribbon, and thread—she even had a craft table.

As they entered the sewing room, Granny told them to close their eyes and hold out their hands. She said, "When I count to three you can open your eyes." "One, two, three!" she said. "Now open your eyes."

They opened their eyes and received a big surprise. Granny made two beautiful patchwork quilts, one for Stacey and one for Paige. The girls were so happy with their quilts that they each gave Granny a big hug.

On the way home, Ms. Grace said she will be taking Paige to meet with her social worker, Mrs. Simpson tomorrow.

"Will I meet with my social worker too?" Stacey asked.

"Not this time," replied Ms. Grace. Paige is going to be reunified with her mother.

"What is reunified?" Stacey asked.

"Reunification is when the local department of social services and your biological parent makes a set of rules for your parents to follow and your parents agree to follow those rules. "Once the rules are followed then the court can grant reunification, which means you can return to your parents," explained Ms. Grace.

"Am I going to be reunified too?" Stacey asked.

"No," said Ms. Grace, "I am hoping to adopt you."

"When will I be adopted?" Stacey asked.

"I don't know," said Ms. Grace.

"Tonight is family night at home and since this is your first family night with us Stacey you get to choose the board games," said Ms. Grace.

"What is family night?" Stacey asked.

"Every Saturday night, we get together as a family and do fun things," said Paige.

"Like what?" Stacey asked.

"First, we take our baths and brush our teeth. "Next, we put on our pajamas." Then, we make hot dogs, smoothies, and pop popcorn, and finally, we choose a board game to play while sitting on the big sofa," said Paige.

The next morning, the girls awaken to the smell of cinnamon toast, bacon, eggs, and hot milk. That smell was coming from the kitchen. It was Ms. Grace cooking breakfast for them.

"Did you girls have a good night's sleep?" asked Ms. Grace.

"Yes," said Stacey.

"Yes," said Paige, "and we had a lot of fun playing board games."

"What did you like most about family night?" Ms. Grace asked Stacey.

"I liked popping popcorn," Stacey said. Can we do it again?

"Soon," replied Ms. Grace. Today Paige is having a visit with her mother and I am taking you to visit Granny after school. Granny said she has a special day planned for you.

"Hello, Stacey," said Granny. Why such a sad face?

"Hello, Granny," said Stacey in her quiet voice. Ms. Grace took Paige on a visit to see her mother.

"I hope she has a wonderful visit with her mother," said Granny.

"So . . . do you think Paige will visit us when she goes to live with her mother?" Stacey asked.

"I think you girls will be able to work out something," said Granny.

"Me too," Stacey replied. "It won't be the same without her."

"Paige will probably have lots to talk about when she returns," said Granny. I have an idea, said Granny! Before we meet Ms. Grace and Paige I am going to take you to the pet shop.

There Stacey met Granny's neighbor, Mr. Rogers. He owned the pet shop. Once inside she saw rabbits, puppies, kittens, gold fish, tropical fish, and canaries.

"What do you like most about the pet shop?" Granny asked.

"I like the canaries because they repeated everything I said," replied Stacey.

After visiting the pet shop, they returned to Granny's house where they met Ms. Grace and Paige. At first it looked like it would be a long ride home, but Granny was right; Paige had plenty to say in the car.

"I had a nice visit with my mother," said Paige. "Next time we will bake a cake," she said. "Then we will watch a movie," Paige added. Can Stacey come on my next visit to meet my mother?" asked Paige.

"We will see," replied Ms. Grace.

As we entered the house, Paige continued. "You will like my mother," said Paige. Just then the phone rang—ring, ring!

It was Mr. Jones! "Hello," said Mr. Jones. "How is Stacey?"

"Hello," said Ms. Grace. "She is doing well."

"I would like to schedule a home visit next Friday to discuss Stacey's adoption," said Mr. Jones.

"We will be here," said Ms. Grace.

Meanwhile, Paige ran upstairs and started packing her overnight bag. She was excited to be going on an overnight home visit to see her mother. She packed her light blue pajamas with the purple polka dots, her cutsie wootsie baby doll, and her toothpaste and toothbrush."

Later that week, Ms. Grace added two pairs of jeans, two shirts, and two sweaters to Paige's suitcase. She also added Paige's pink-and-gray dress, pink stockings, and Sunday shoes.

"I will miss Paige," said Stacey.

"And she will miss you too," said Ms. Grace.

"It was early in the morning when Paige woke up yelling, It's Friday, it's Friday!"

After Ms. Grace drove Paige to meet Mrs. Simpson, Mr. Jones came to their house to speak with Ms. Grace about Stacey's adoption. .

Hello Stacey he said, "I heard you have a new bicycle,"

"Yes," said Stacey. "My bicycle is pink; it has two big wheels, one in the front of my bike and one in the back of my bike. It also has two small wheels, one on the left side of my bike and one on the right side of my bike."

"Those are called training wheels," said Ms. Grace. I am taking Stacey to the park to teach her how to ride her bike.

"I hope you have fun, Stacey" said Mr. Jones.

Mr. Jones told Ms. Grace that the request for Stacey's adoption was approved and she will receive a letter in the mail.

"That's great," said Ms. Grace. We will check the mail daily.

As Ms. Grace walked Mr. Jones to the door, the phone rang. It's Mrs. Cox; Mrs. Cox is Ms. Grace's best friend. Ms. Grace was supposed to call Mrs. Cox when Mr. Jones left, but she was so excited about the request for Stacey's adoption being approved that she forgot.

"I am so excited for you both," said Mrs. Cox. "We must celebrate."

"Yes," said Ms. Grace, "we will as soon as the adoption is finalized."

"What is finalized?" Stacey asked.

"Finalized mean once the judge says you are mine and I am yours then there is nothing else for us to do," said Ms. Grace, "except be a family."

"Then we are together forever?" asked Stacey.

"Yes," said Ms. Grace, "we are together forever."

After Stacey ate lunch, Ms. Grace took her to the park to teach her how to ride her bicycle.

"You will need to wear your helmet," said Ms. Grace and I will wear my helmet too.

"Why should we wear a helmet?" Stacey asked.

"For safety," said Ms. Grace.

"You mean if I fall off my bike and hit my head, the helmet will protect me?" Stacey asked.

"Yes," said Ms. Grace, "the helmet can safeguard your head."

At first, Stacey was scared to ride her bike, but Ms. Grace said she would hold the bike so Stacey can sit on the seat. Then she held the handlebars while Stacey put her feet on the pedals. Next she walked along side of the bike as Stacey pushed down on the pedals. Finally, she let Stacey go and off she went.

"Stacey, you're doing it!" yelled Ms. Grace. "You're actually riding your bike."

"Yeah!" Stacey yelled. "I'm riding my bike, oh . . . oh . . . oh . . ." She fell in the grass.

"Are you okay?" asked Ms. Grace.

"Yes," said Stacey. Ms. Grace was right; my helmet stopped me from hurting my head and my bicycle was okay too. It only had a few scratches on the handlebars.

As Ms. Grace drove home from the park, she said, they were going for a ride on an elevator to visit her friend Mrs. Cox, she lives on the eleventh floor of the Wiltshire Apartments". When they entered Mrs. Cox apartment, Mrs. Cox greeted them with a smile.

"Hello, Stacey," said Mrs. Cox.

"Hello," replied Stacey.

"Can I get you something cold to drink?" Mrs. Cox asked.

"No, thank you," they replied.

"Stacey would you like to see the balcony?" asked Mrs. Cox.

"Yes," replied Stacey. "You have a nice view."

"Thank you," said Mrs. Cox. "I lived in this same apartment since I was a little girl;" Mrs. Grace and I have been best friends since the third grade."

"How did you meet?" Stacey asked.

"We met while walking our dogs in the park," replied Mrs. Cox.

"I have a best friend too," Stacey said. "Her name is Paige." "Do you think Paige and I will remain best friends, like you and Ms. Grace?"

"I don't see why not," said Mrs. Cox. "You should write Paige a letter telling her how you feel."

"I think I will," replied Stacey.

Later that evening, Ms. Grace gave me a pencil and paper. "What should I say in the letter to Paige?" asked Stacey.

"Write whatever is in your heart," replied Ms. Grace.

"I know, I'll start with Dear Paige."

Dear Paige,

I am very happy that you are going to live with your mother.

I hope you can visit me and I can visit you.

We will be best friends forever and ever, and nothing is ever going to change that.

I will miss you.

Your best friend,

Stacey

"I hope Paige will like the letter I wrote," said Stacey.

"I'm sure she will just love it," said Ms. Grace.

"I can't wait until Paige comes home so I can give her the letter," Stacey said.

While Ms. Grace made breakfast, Stacey waited near the front door for Paige to come home.

"No dear, Paige will be home this afternoon," said Ms. Grace.

"Can we bake Paige a cake?" Stacey asked.

"It's not her birthday," said Ms. Grace. I know," said Ms. Grace, "what about giving Paige a farewell party?

"Then can we bake Paige a cake?" asked Stacey.

"Yes, we can bake Paige a cake for the party," said Ms. Grace.

As Stacey was talking to Ms. Grace the doorbell rang. "It must be Paige and her social worker, Mrs. Simpson," said Ms. Grace.

"Oh no it was the mailman!" said Stacey.

"I have mail for Ms. Grace," said the mailman.

It was the letter from Family Court that read:

Family Court of the State

County of the Borough

In the Matter of the Adoption of Stacey W.

You are hereby noticed that the adoption hearing for the above named child will be held on the fifteenth of this month, at 10:00 a.m., at the Family Court of the State, located at 123 ABC Street of the state.

Please feel free to contact your caseworker, Mr. Jones, regarding your appearance. Failure to appear may waive your opportunity to adopt the above named child.

Verified

By this state and the judge of this state

After reading the letter, Ms. Grace told Stacey the adoption hearing was in a few weeks.

"I can't wait to tell Paige about my court date," Stacey said.

Just then the doorbell rang. It was Mrs. Simpson and Paige.

Stacey hurried to Paige when she saw her coming in the house. "Guess what we got in the mail?" she asked.

"What?" Paige asked.

The letter. . .the letter! Stacey shouted.

While Ms. Grace spoke with Mrs. Simpson, Stacey ran up the stairs and Paige went to get her suitcase.

"I have a gift for you," Stacey said to Paige.

"I have a gift for you too," said Paige.

"You girls can exchange gifts after you eat your lunch," Ms. Grace said.

As they continued to talk, Mrs. Simpson told Ms. Grace, "Paige will be going to live with her mother on Friday."

"Will you be picking Paige up or should I bring her to your office?" asked Ms. Grace.

"I will pick her up at 7:00 p.m. Friday night," said Mrs. Simpson.

"OK," said Ms. Grace as she walked Mrs. Simpson to the door, "We will give Paige a farewell party."

Stacey and Paige each said they would count to three before they exchanged gifts.

One, two, three!

Stacey gave Paige a blue envelope, and Paige gave Stacey a pink envelope.

"Who will read their letter first?" asked Ms. Grace.

"I will," said Paige.

Paige read Stacey's letter and gave her a big hug. She said, "We will always be best friends."

Next, Stacey read Paige's letter.

It read:

Dear Stacey,

I always wanted a little sister, just like you.

You are also my best friend and nothing is ever going to change that.

I will write you, and I hope you will write to me.

I will always love you.

Your big sister,

Paige

While Stacey and Paige were playing with their dolls, Ms. Grace called Granny and Mrs. Cox to invite them to Paige's farewell party.

"I will be there," said Granny.

"I will not miss it," said Mrs. Cox.

After making the list of things to do for the party, Ms. Grace whispered to Stacey, "What kind of cake do you want to bake for Paige's farewell party?"

"Can we bake Paige red velvet cupcakes with vanilla frosting instead?" whispered Stacey.

"I will buy the ingredients when I go food shopping tomorrow," said Ms. Grace.

"Can we go food shopping too?" Stacey asked.

"Remember it's a surprise for Paige," replied Ms. Grace, "and you girls will be in school."

"Can we go to Granny's house tomorrow?" Stacey asked.

"Yes," said Ms. Grace, "Granny would love for you girls to visit her after school."

After school, Ms. Grace took Stacey and Paige to Granny's house, while she went to the market.

While Paige was in the kitchen making lemonade, Granny asked Stacey if Paige knew about the party?"

"No! We want it to be a surprise." said Stacey.

"How are you going to surprise Paige?" asked Granny.

"Ms. Grace will pick Paige up after school and take her to her dance lessons on Friday. Then, she will take her to the pet shop to see Mr. Rogers," she is buying Paige a pet as a going away present," Stacey replied.

"How are you feeling now that Paige will be leaving us?" asked Granny.

Stacey told Granny that she was sad at first that Paige was leaving them, but now she is happy because they can write and visit each other.

"I am happy you girls found a way to stay in touch with each other," said Granny.

While we were in the garden with Granny, Ms. Grace arrived.

"Did you invite Mrs. Cox?" Stacey whispered.

"Yes," Ms. Grace replied. Mrs. Cox was invited to the party," she said, she will bring the fruit punch, Granny will bring the chips and dip, Mr. Rogers will bring the balloons, and I will make the cupcakes.

"Paige is going to be so surprised," said Stacey. "I think this is going to be the best surprise ever."

A few days later, Paige said good-bye to her classmates, Maty, Josh, Kassi and her teacher Mrs. Pemberton.

"I am going to miss you all," said Paige.

"We will miss you too," said Mrs. Pemberton.

"Remember to write," said Maty.

"I will," replied Paige.

"I know," said Kassi, "we should take a picture together."

"We can hang it in the classroom so we could remember Paige," said Josh.

"Good idea," said Mrs. Pemberton, "I will call your parents and ask them for permission to take a picture of you with your classmate because she is leaving us today."

Later that afternoon, Paige and her classmates took pictures together before Ms. Grace picked her up from school.

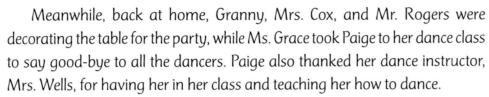

Meanwhile, back at home, Granny, Mrs. Cox, and Mr. Rogers were decorating the table for the party, while Ms. Grace took Paige to her dance class to say good-bye to all the dancers. Paige also thanked her dance instructor, Mrs. Wells, for having her in her class and teaching her how to dance.

"You were a good student," said Mrs. Wells. "I hope you continue to dance."

On the way home, Paige said she loved dancing school and wanted to be a prima ballerina.

"Can you show me how to dance like a ballerina when we get home?" asked Ms. Grace.

"Me too," asked Stacey.

Paige was so excited about teaching them how to dance the ballet that as soon as they arrived home; she jumped out of the car, ran up the steps, and pushed open the front door.

"Surprise! Surprise! Surprise!" they yelled.

"What's going on?" asked Paige.

"Surprise," Stacey said, "this is your going-away party."

During the party, they laughed and took pictures; they even listened to music, while Mr. Rogers danced with Granny. They ate so much that their bellies were almost full, until Granny gave everyone some cupcakes and fruit punch."

Ding dong, the doorbell rang; it was Mrs. Simpson, Paige's social worker. "Come in," said Ms. Grace. "Won't you join us?"

Paige brought Mrs. Simpson a cupcake. She said it was from her surprise party.

"Thank you," said Mrs. Simpson

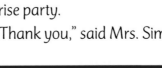

While Mrs. Simpson and Ms. Grace talked in the kitchen, Paige and Stacey said their good-byes.

"Remember to write," said Paige.

"I will," replied Stacey.

Granny took us by the hand and said, "You girls realize that although you will be living apart you will always be family."

"Yes," said Paige and Stacey.

As Mrs. Simpson and Paige drove away, we all waved so long.

"Paige looked like she had a good time at her surprise party," said Ms. Grace.

"Did you have a good time, Stacey?" Granny asked.

"Yes, I did, Granny," Stacey replied. "Granny invited me to stay the night at her house. May I?"

"Yes," replied Ms. Grace, "Granny will make hot chocolate and tell stories."

"Will you put lots and lots of whipped cream on top?" Stacey asked Granny.

"For you I will," replied Granny.

On the way to Granny's house, we saw a shooting star. "Did you make a wish?" asked Granny.

"I don't know what to wish for," Stacey replied.

"Close your eyes and think of something special," said Granny.

"OK," replied Stacey, "I made my wish."

"Did you keep your eyes closed?" asked Granny.

"Yes," Stacey replied. "Do you think my wish will come true?"

"We will see," said Granny, "we will see."

Finally, Stacey arrived at Granny's house. Stacey was beginning to think her wish was never going to come true, but then the phone rang.

"It's for you, Stacey," said Granny.

"Hello," Stacey answered.

"Hello," said the caller.

"It's Paige," Stacey said. "It's Paige," she squealed.

Later that evening, Granny and Stacey enjoyed chocolate milk with lots of whipped cream.

"Did you girls have lots to talk about?" Granny asked.

"Yes, we did," said Stacey. "I was beginning to think I would never hear from Paige, but then I made a wish that Paige would call and she did."

Suddenly, Stacey remembered that in a few weeks she was going to court with Ms. Grace.

"Have you ever been to court?" Stacey asked Granny.

"No!" said Granny. "But I've seen court on television."

"Will you come with us?" Stacey asked.

"I wish I could," said Granny, "but I have some errands to run."

As Stacey waited for Ms. Grace to pick her up from school she tried doing her class work, but she could not; She was too busy thinking about going to court and having a mommy.

"How does it feel to have a mommy?" Stacey asked her classmates.

"My mother makes me feel nurtured and protected," said one student.

"And my mother makes me feel comforted and loved," said another.

Stacey listened with wonder as her classmates spoke. She wondered how she was going to feel when she gets a mommy.

"What if Ms. Grace doesn't want to be my mommy anymore?" she wondered. Then she remembered she had a biological mother, a foster mother, and now she is going to have an adoptive mother.

The bell rang and it was now lunchtime. Stacey knew Ms. Grace was coming to pick her up after recess, and recess was right after lunch, so she packed her book bag and met Ms. Grace in the main office.

"How was school?" Ms. Grace asked.

"Good," Stacey replied.

"Did you eat your lunch?" asked Ms. Grace.

"Yes," Stacey said, "we had chicken squares."

"All rise!" said the bailiff.

"Good morning," said Judge Mason, "you may be seated."

"Today we are here in the matter of Stacey's adoption," said Judge Mason. Are all parties present?

"Yes," said Mrs. Lewis his assistant. The lawyer, Mr. Waters; the social worker, Mr. Jones; and her adoptive parent, Ms. Grace, is present, as well as Stacey, you're honor.

"Since all parties are present, we may begin," said Judge Mason. "It appears that your application for adoption is in order."

"Yes," replied Mr. Waters.

Judge Mason asked Ms. Grace, "Do you resolve to maintain a safe, nurturing, and permanent home for Stacey within your loving family?"

"I do," Ms. Grace replied.

"Do you understand that you will have full parental rights and all legal responsibilities to Stacey?" asked Judge Mason.

"Yes," replied Ms. Grace.

Then the judge wrote on the court order.

"By virtue of the authority vested in me by the Constitution and the laws of the United States, do hereby proclaim Stacey W. to be now known as Stacey F. in witness whereof, I have hereunto set my hand this Adoption day in November,"

Judge Mason

After the judge granted the application of the adoption of Stacey F., Mrs. Lewis spoke with Ms. Grace. "You will receive an adoption order together with your adoption certificate showing you are now Stacey's mother and Stacey is your daughter," she said.

"Since the order was granted, we will have a short ceremony of congratulation for the family," said Mrs. Lewis as she led them to the family room at court.

Meanwhile, Granny was home planning a party for Stacey to officially welcome her into the family. Mrs. Cox was also there to help with the party; she was setting the table, while Paige was there making a collage of pictures, and Mr. Rogers was blowing up the balloons.

When Stacey arrived home, everyone yelled surprise!

"Welcome home, Stacey F.!" everyone yelled. "Welcome home to your family."

"Stacey was so happy to be adopted that she ran to her mother Ms. Grace and gave her a big hug and said "I have a Ma, a Mom, and a Mommy, and they made National Adoption Day special for me."

41

Printed in the United States
By Bookmasters